A Capricious Breeze

Farzana Lisa Hussain

Published 2010 by arima publishing
www.arimapublishing.com

ISBN 978 1 84549 450 6

© Farzana Lisa Hussain 2010

Printed and bound in the United Kingdom

Typeset in Garamond 11/14

Swirl is an imprint of arima publishing.

arima publishing
ASK House, Northgate Avenue
Bury St Edmunds, Suffolk IP32 6BB
t: (+44) 01284 700321
www.arimapublishing.com

The story this novel portrays is that no matter how rich or poor you are, and whatever part of the world you live in, you might be the victim of abuse, neglect and torment. The characters in the work are entirely fictitious and represent the everyday people we might meet and pass by on the street. It is the common life story of the world.

For my parents.

Today who I am is because of them.
My success is their success of being the best parents.
Mum and Dad thank you for giving us the beautiful life.

Mr and Mrs Salman

A breakfast table is set up for five persons: father and mother occupy two chairs, the other three are vacant.

"It is such a beautiful morning, and they all are sleeping?" said Mrs Salman with bitter feelings. "You have spoiled them. They all don't listen to me. I wish I had never given birth to these children."

"Why on earth did I marry you in the first place?"

By this time she had become furious, "Why, it would be better …" with a deep, breath she speaks again, "It would be better if you give poison and kill me! You will be free to do anything you like".

There was silence for a minute. Mrs Salman had a few sips of coffee to quench her thirst; Mr Salman sat at the head of the table. He was pretending to read the newspaper. To avoid Mrs Salman's threatening look, he held his newspaper in a certain way that worked as a screen. That made Mrs Salman more annoyed with him. She got up from the chair snatched the paper, and tore it into small pieces. Mr Salman was shocked and speechless at his wife's behaviour.

Mrs Salman was red with anger and began with a tone that would make a lion leave the room, "From the time I married you, you never gave me any peaceful life. You made me exhausted through entertaining your greedy friends and relatives. When I married you, I was young and did not know anything about matrimonial life. Now, I am a mother of three fully-grown girls.

You never take care of the children! Nor do you notice anything for the home! I would have divorced you, but I didn't! Only for the sake of our daughters.

The last sentences stabbed Mr Salman right into his heart. He rose from his chair and stood before his wife. In that moment he was capable of doing anything to his wife, but he did not do it. He didn't want to commit a crime.

"All these times, I was controlling my anger, but now I cannot do it any more, he exclaimed. You're the housewife. It is your duty to take care of the children and home: That is why I married you! You should be grateful to me. No you are unhappy instead. I have given jewellery, three or four cars, and a big house with servants, to do all the housework. I even take you abroad with me every year. Just tell me how many people in Bangladesh can afford all these luxuries that I have given you?"

"I spit at your richness! She actually spat on the food that was lying on the table. You never spend much on charity. The only time, you gave a big amount of money to the poor was when there was a flood disaster. That's because you wanted to be famous. I'm telling you … a day will come when your money won't help you".

"Enough of your insane talking! Today you've proved yourself a hypocrite. My wish is to send you and my three daughters to London. It's going to be the best for both of us. Oh…besides that, you have no right to be telling how to spend my money. At least, I help the poor and I don't care if it is a little amount or not! And I must warn you that there is no need to discuss today's altercation with our daughters. You know it affects them mentally: Especially Jeasmine".

Mr Salman did not wait for his wife's answer. He opened the dining room door and as he marched out of the room. He forcefully slammed the door behind him; if it was a glass door it would have shattered. Alone, Mrs Salman fell onto a chair, helpless and alone.

Jeasmine

6th May 1993

I could not believe it, my dad is seriously sending us to London. We are going next month. My dad told me, he wont allow me back to Bangladesh until I finish all my education.

My family, they are very conservative and I don't know how I am going to live my life in London.

Mrs Salman and Reasmine

"Mum, why did dad make a sudden plan like this? Aren't we happy here in Bangladesh? And don't you think that Western Culture is going to be very fast for Jeasmine?" exclaimed Reasmine.

"I don't know anything! Don't ask me! You know that we are all forbidden to say anything against you fathers wishes. And, besides it would be better for us. Your father will appreciate our value, even if he does not see all the time. I am not worried about you and Neasmine. Neasmine is 20 years old and she knows the difference between bad and good. Jeasmine is daddy's girl", said Mrs Salman with an annoyed voice, "Your father has spoiled her. I don't like the friends she mixed with. Sometimes I am worried about Jeasmine. I have to be more strict with her when we go to London, and put her in a strict school".

Jeasmine

17th Oct 1993

I am in London now. Life in London is not boring. I haven't made any close friends yet; soon I'll make some. I don't miss my dad very much because he was always busy outside. He spent his time alone in his room when he was at home. I miss my friends, especially, when I see other girls here having fun with their friends.

I hope my dad will come and stay with us. I care about my dad more than anything else. I came to London with new hope, when I go back I can go as a new leaf.

20th Oct 1993

Life in London is an extravaganza. I like our four bedroom flat in Kendal Street. And even more pleasant, there is a chemist shop, where a handsome boy sits at the cashier desk. He speaks perfect English.

Love at first sight, I call it. Oh he is simply gorgeous. Before I could only see these kinds of boys in movies; now this is face to face, it's like a dream. From the moment I saw him I was crazy for him. Every night I think of him, I hope some day he and I will be friends.

26th Oct 1993

Today my two sisters, Reasmine and Neasmine, have somehow found out about my love life. Being the youngest, I have to endure this alone.

My mum was hysterical about the matter, I got assault and battery, from my mum. My crime was that I am 15 years old and I am not allowed to be in love at this age (in my family). If I do it again, my mum will take me back to the village on the next available flight.

27th Oct 1993

I woke at 10 o'clock in the morning and after I finished my breakfast, I studied until noon. Then in the afternoon my mum went out and we three sisters stayed at home. I watched TV a little bit. I didn't go out all day.

When my mum came home she gave me £20, to buy something for myself. She gave the money to make me happy, after yesterday's incident. I was very glad to get outside. Neasmine went with me. We passed the chemist shop where my Romeo used to be, and went to the newsagent's shop next to it. I didn't dare to attempt to look inside the chemists; I know what offensive punishment would befall me.

To see his face used to make me very happy. I loved him, but he doesn't know and he will never know, because I did not have the courage to tell him.

20th Oct 1993

Another boring day. I didn't go out. I watched all the boring programmes on television. At night Reasmine went out alone to a party. I guess she is allowed because she is 22 years.

I'll be very happy when the holiday is over because I can go out every day when my school is open.

I feel really bored at home.

30th Oct 1993

I watched TV all morning, before anyone woke up. Then, in the afternoon, we all went to Knightsbridge for shopping.

In the evening it was really boring; mum watched Hindi language films on the VCR. Neasmine and Reasmine slept in their room. I was waiting for the six o'clock news on BBC.

In the meantime there was nothing for me to do. To pass the time I just stood beside the window and watched the people on the street.

The worst thing is, I don't have any friends at school nor outside school. With friends I could go anywhere I like and whenever I like. I need friends sometime, it is good not to have too many friends, but I don't have a single friend. On the coming Monday our school opens and I am looking forward to it. I feel really bored at home. The only things I am allowed to do at home is to eat, sleep and study; it is like a prison.

10th Nov 1993

Our history teacher died yesterday morning. Miss A Smith died from brain haemorrhage. I feel sad for her and little bit guilty inside my heart. When I had my first history lesson with her, I thought she is the only teacher I don't like: I was scared of her.

Now she will never teach us again. God please forgive me ...... for what I thought about her. I pray to god, that she will rest in peace forever.

11th Nov 1993

In school things didn't go well. I found out that some of the girls laugh at me and make fun of me, behind my back. I felt very sad, and because I could not tell anyone about it I felt very heavy inside my heart.

At home everything went wrong, also. My mum scolded me for not doing any housework. I wish I was back in my country where there are service people to do the housework.

I don't know what I should do first; my homework or clean my bedroom?

13th Nov 1993

I am happy, my dad is coming to visit next Sunday. Everything is going smoothly at school, but not at home.

I am very lonely, I need a friend and I don't care if it is a boy or a girl. I lost the boy I loved. I still dream of him but he is lost forever in real life.

Sometimes I feel that something is missing in my life. Maybe it's dad. No it can't be because he phones every week. I don't know what is really missing in my jigsaw puzzle life "je ne sais pas?"

25th Nov 1993

On Sunday the 21st November, my dad came to London. My dad brought lots of frozen curry from home. My dad was very happy to see us and we were also happy to see dad, even my mum was happy. For the first time, my parents didn't fight.

Well, happiness did not last long. Daddy left today for Bangladesh at half past five in the evening. He went to airport with his friend. I felt like an orphan, when he got into the car and drove off. I feel like crying, whenever I remember that scene.

26th Nov 1993

We were having our art class today when a few girls asked me weird questions, like having children and then getting married, and to fall in love with boys. All I said is that I hated this stuff and I meant it! But they don't want to believe it and so they keep on asking me, treating me as if I was interesting case.

I cannot follow their path because I come from a culture where to talk about sex is a sin. The last few days my dad preached to us; I must study hard, achieve better results and then think of other things in life.

If I tell my sisters and my mum that some of the girls in my year talk about sex, I am sure they will beat me, for mixing with those girls. The reason they had put me in a private girls' school was to avoid these situations.

1 Dec 1993

We are changing our flat this Wednesday and I am looking forward to it. I never dreamt that I would go to live in the area where once Sherlock Holmes had lived. Wait till I tell this to all my friends in Bangladesh.

I bought four *'horror point'* books, which is a secret to everyone at home.

Life at school is normal. Sometimes I feel sad and I don't know why. I really miss my friends back there.

3rd Dec 1993

In my geography group there is a girl named Faye. She is pretty, talented, smart and popular. God had made her perfect and there is no doubt about it. I feel sad and jealous when I see her. She is good at art and other subjects. She also does ballet dancing. She even had a beautiful figure and she speaks gracefully.

Maybe jealous is not the right word. When I see her it makes me want to kill myself. I may be rich in my country, but I'm 'just' well off here in London.

'Why could I not be perfect like her?'

4th Dec 1993

Today I felt desperately sad for all my good friends in Bangladesh. While I was looking at photos of my friends, and their autographs, it made me feel like crying.

I wonder if they think of me? I don't care if they don't miss me, but I really do miss them, and I wont tell anyone about this. Life in Bangladesh was really fun. I'll never forget those days, those fun filled memories and those happy feelings.

It will take time to build these relationships here; I wonder how long it will take? I am ready to bend on my knees to anyone for friendship.

10th Dec 1993

I am in our new flat. We moved on 8th, Wednesday. I was so excited about it, but the worst thing was that I had to pack a lot.

Sometimes I miss Kendal St and sometimes I am glad to leave it behind. It has given me pain, that 'chemist boy', whose name I don't know, and how my family, misunderstood me. They thought I was contradicting to them; I'll never ever talk about another guy in front of my family.

18th Dec 1993

I didn't go out today. My mum threw a small party at our place. It was quite boring.

Last night I dreamt of my relatives in Bangladesh and they were thinking of me and missing me.

I also dreamt of my best friend Rosey. I hope she got my card that I posted to her.

Each day I am having a boring day. Our flat is pretty but it seems to me like a sophisticated prison.

23rd Dec 1993

I am not happy. My report card with my exams was posted to my parents.

My mum was very angry, as were my two older sisters. They are the ones who encouraged my mum to be angry with me. Especially Reasmine … she is a mean sister.

Oh! My days are going horribly wrong. They are making me insane, crazy. I just don't know when to cry and when to laugh. I have no one to support me. I don't know what wrong I have done in my past life that I have to suffer so now.

If I do anything good, they will not give me any credit, nor will they tell me that it was a good thing I had done. However, if I do anything wrong then they are onto me like a tornado. I just don't understand them!

My dad is not here with us, and I can't complain to him on the phone. None of my sisters support me, nor does my mum. If I do complain to my father he never scolds anyone, but instead he will think I am the guilty one.

If I die, no one will want to remember me. I just want to be banished. I don't want to stay in this universe, nor in heaven or hell. I know even evil will not like me.

If god does not like me, then no one will like me. I am a hopeless child. I should not have been born. I am useless. Nobody cares for me.

25th Dec 1993

Christmas time! Although I don't celebrate Christmas, I share the spirit of the Christmas season.

In my bedroom I turn off the light and look through the window. I can see my neighbours' Christmas tree. How beautifully they have decorated it. At this time of the year everybody all over the world, spends time with their family.

I wish my father was here with us in London.

31st Dec 1993

We are going to a dinner party. A friend of our family has invited us all.

I can't believe that we are spending our New Year in England, I mean in London. I miss my dad, if only he was with us in London. Then it would have been a different new year. I wonder what he is doing alone back home? Oh! God bring peace to my family and to the world. This New Year time, I'll never forget because I've never spent a New Year before without my father nor outside of Bangladesh.

Tête-À-Tête

The sun was shining bright, the young and old enjoying the summer weather. The seduction of summer pulled everyone outdoors. Even Jeasmine couldn't resist the temptation. She went to Hyde Park alone, to refresh her mind. Jeasmine got bored of staying at home, and studying in her holidays. It's been three months since she came to London but she not happy.

Jeasmine was walking slowly, head down and arms wrapped around her breast. The cool summer breeze playing with her dyed chestnut brown hair. She did not notice the people around her, she just walked straight to where her two eyes took her. Suddenly she realised that she no longer could hear the noises and laughter of the people. She looked around; she was not sure which part of the park she was in now.

There were a few couples around the area. She did not go towards them, because they were busy being intimate.

From a distance she saw a man who was sitting on a park bench. Jeasmine asked when she was standing front of him, "can you please tell me what time is it?"

The man did not answer. Jeasmine observed him for few minutes. His eyes were sullen, he looked tired as if he hadn't slept for months. His features were mixed. He must have mixed parents. His mother might be white and his father might be Jamaican possibly.

After a short pause, in a wistful manner he began …

"I'm sorry are you talking to me?"

"Well can you see anyone near you, except me?"

"No, the point is, I couldn't believe that after a week. I heard someone talking to me"

"That's sad don't you have any friends?"

"I used to, but I'll meet them again, when I've money".

"Don't you have any home or family?"

"I used to have both, happy ones!"

"Are you alone in this world?"

"Actually I do have a so called mother and father".

"Then why don't you go to them?"

"They got divorced when I was 12, because my father had an affair with his secretary. Mum moved to a council flat four years ago. She lost her job, and she had to take care of five more children. Now I am obliged to come out on street. You're crying?"

"Sorry I couldn't help it! It's too much for me", inside her heart Jeasmine thought … how could people in a developed country like England, suffer? All through her life she had known that in Western countries there is no poverty. The pocket money a child gets in Britain is more than a labourers wage in Bangladesh. Jeasmine was touched by his story, and with a kind smile she began

"What's your name?"

"Mark and yours?"

Jeasmine quickly thought of a name.

"Sarah", she said in a hurried tone, "Oh, can you please tell me what the time is?"

"Five minutes to 1 pm".

"How time flies. Talking to you made me forget that I have to go home!"

"Where do you live?"

Again she was in a quandary. This time without taking time, she said, "Maida-Vale, I think I should be going now". She looked at his face: her eyes met his eyes. One little glance hypnotised her. She was under a spell. "Do you need money?" she said in a shy voice, "I can help you".

Mark was surprised to hear that, "How can you help me?" he exclaimed, "you, yourself a young person, probably younger than me".

"To help someone, you don't need to be old. The question is do you need it or not? And besides I'm also in pain like you. I know how you feel".

"Then I can take you to an enchanted world, if only you've the money" said Mark, and with excitement he rose on his feet from his sitting position, and reached out his right arm to shake hands with Jeasmine.

With courtesy, they both shook hands, but inside Jeasmine's body she felt Mark's fingers as a leech, like he was sucking the blood from her body.

Peregrination to End

"You mustn't be friendly with everyone in there!" whispered Mark into Jeasmine's ear.

She did not hear properly, what Mark just said. She did not try to hear it again. Jeasmine was busy observing the area, she was surrounded by. She looked around; she could see no human soul in sight. 'The area looked like a garbage dump' thought Jeasmine, 'after all I live in a posh part of the city'. In front of Jeasmine and Mark stood a two story building, which looked in disrepair, abandoned and any minute it might collapse. 'In the Victorian period this building would have been the pride of some factory owner' thought Jeasmine silently. The word Victorian took Jeasmine to a dreamland. A land where Jeasmine was not Jeasmine. There she had no ethnic background. She could transplant herself the way she wanted to be. She would be a person of different character; as if she was from 18th century, but not 20th century.

"Are you alright? You seemed stone cold," said Mark taking Jeasmine's hands into his.

Mark's voice brought her back to the present time. "No, I'm fine. I was just thinking about how this place would have looked in Victorian times" said Jeasmine with a deep breath that she released with each word she pronounced.

"Do you like to live in Victorian times?" asked Mark.

"Do I? Oh god! I would just love to be back in those days. Everything in the Victorian period fascinates me, the clothes, the cultures, the people, lifestyles, you name it", said Jeasmine.

"Well Sarah you can make your dream come true," said Mark. "When he called Jeasmine by the name 'Sarah', she felt guilty. Guilty for not telling him the truth. 'What is the use of telling him my real name, I don't like my real name anyway. It is one of those names which remains me, from where I am and who I am', thought Jeasmine in her head. "Really", said Jeasmine as she quickly realised, that Mark was expecting an answer from her.

"Just wait till we enter this building", said Mark, as he was talking he brought a key from his jeans pocket. He unlocked the pad lock with his key and then opened the door wide for Jeasmine.

Hand in hand Jeasmine entered with Mark. The pair looked as like Hansel and Gretel entering the witch's house.

15th Jan 1994

Jeasmine:

Today (from school) a good friend of mine came to visit me. She is the only friend I had made at that time. Victoria, who helped me to face the other girls in school. She helps me with my studies and gives me encouragement. Now, I see things differently. Four months ago, I was lonely, not anymore; Victoria is now here to give me support.

17th Jan 1994

Today I discovered something extraordinary. I could not believe my eyes, when I first saw my discovery. It all happened when I woke up late in the morning. I looked at the clock it was 20 minutes to nine. Nine is the registration time; I knew if I do not hurry I will be late for school.

I quickly dressed up, grabbed a banana and within a minute I was crossing Melbourne Street. It was going to take 15 minutes to get to my school. I did not wait for a cab. I knew a short cut, which I had never used it; today I was definitely going to take it. I went through T Street; one of my best friends lives there. Then I came to Harley Street. Whenever I walk through Harley Street I think of how this street looked in 19th century. I looked at each house as I passed by.

I was over the moon, when I saw Elizabeth Barrett Browning's house. I could not believe it. I really passed a poet's house whose poem was in our textbook. I told my English teacher Mrs Walker about my discovery when I had my lesson with her that day.

Now I have decided to pass E.B.B's house everyday, whenever I go to school. The house needs renovating badly. I figured out that nobody lives there. It looks gloomy and cold from outside and inside there were no curtains and no furniture. I am not get scared to imagine that some day I might see Elizabeth Barrett Browning's spirit. I would welcome her; maybe even make her my close friend. I'll tell her to help me with my education.

If only I could meet her spirit. When I become wealthy in my own right, I will buy her house and treasure it.

18th Jan 1994

Today I again passed Elizabeth's house. I don't know, but I have begun to feel that I could see her. I even talk to her, whenever I pass her house. I had tea with her in her lovely parlour. I usually have long conversations with her. I talked about my problems and she always listens to me.

I even tell her about how I spent my day. I also asked her to help me with my English. I do not know how, but she might be helping me, because my English is actually improving.

To me she seems very kind person. I can hear her when she speaks with me. She is a human being to me. All this happen as I pass her house; it is only a few seconds walk but to me it seems an hour or so.

The Ramadan is coming. That is why we went to Wembley to do the grocery shopping.

I did not want to go. I don't like the atmosphere there. It feels to me that I am not in England. I don't like the Indian sub-continent's cultures and I am sorry for that. I wish I was never born at all. Why is our country not rich like England? Why is our country is only known for flooding? If our country had been richer than England, then they would not have discriminated us Asians.

15th Feb 1994

I could not believe that our school Principal made space for praying, for those who are Muslim, because of the Ramadan.

I could never have imagined that I would be praying in school especially in a Christian country.

25th Feb 1994

Last Friday Ramadan started. I fasted today and it was quite a tiring task; while fasting, I had to play netball at school. If I complain I will not be able to fast. This is the first time my dad is not with us during the Ramadan.

2nd Mar 1994

We are in New York, we came yesterday. We have been doing lots of shopping. New York is an exciting city, but not safe, also it is very unclean.

In my life I have never seen it snow that hard. New York is a fun place but as a city London's extraordinary. London has hidden charms and that few can find. Not only London, the whole UK has an enchanted charm which I have found and I cherish.

4th Mar 1994

Reasmine and Neasmine went out late at night, when my mother was sleeping. If our mum had found out they would have been dead. I did not go, I stayed at the hotel. I don't even know when they came home.

It is funny, people don't believe us when we say we are Bangladeshi. Maybe we dress differently, more Westernly, or maybe we look different to other Bangladeshi. It could be we spend too much money on expensive things.

6th Mar 1994

We came back to London at 7 o'clock in the morning. I am glad to be far from the sky scrappers and traffic. New York scares me, the ultra modernisation makes me feel that soon we the people of this planet going to end in war and hate.

13th Mar 1994

Today was our Eid day. Thank god! I didn't have to miss school. My dad could not be here because of his business. He was not here last month for my birthday. I miss my dad. My dad had sent £100 for each of us on occasion of Eid, as a present, it is a tradition of Islam culture.

31st Mar 1994

I did survey at Regent's Park for my geography course work. I feel very happy to study in this country. The education system is very enjoyable. I am glad to be outside home. At least I don't have to be bullied by my mum and sisters. I miss my dad. He called yesterday and he is coming soon to see us. If my dad was here he would have been proud of me.

11th April 1994

Aya, my other friend after Victoria, came to see me and see how I was doing with my survey. I met her at Regent's Park. She told me after her GCSE exams are finished, she will probably go back to her home in Japan.

I felt sad hearing this, because we were just getting to know each other well. I'll miss her. I think I'll be leaving this country after I finish my studies. There will be only the memories to stay with me forever. No matter whether they are sad or happy ones.

12th April 1994

My two good friends (from school) came to see me. Actually I have invited them to our flat. My mum had prepared Asian food for them. I was worried that if they could not make it, my mum would be very angry with me. Then next time my mum would not allow me to brings friends at our flat.

I was really happy they came, it proved they're not using me, but they're true friends to me. I hope we'll always be friends.

14th April 1994

When my dad rang the bell I thought it might be the postman. I was surprised to see my dad, that early in the morning. I thought I was dreaming. Everything is different with a dad around. To me, my dad is the best dad in the whole wide world.

17th April 1994

Today my dad left. After he left the house, I shut myself in my room and I cried till my eyes hurt. I hope god will take him back to Bangladesh safely. Why is England so far from Bangladesh? Why could London not be a mile drive from my home city, Dhaka in Bangladesh?

Every time my dad comes and goes back, I'm stressed. What if anything happens to the plane? God forbids me to think of such things. My dad is the person I love. If anything happens to him I'm going to die, because when my dad is not around my mum tortures me. Nobody cares for me except my dad.

25th April 1994

For Trinity term, we start a new sport at school called 'rounders'. It is not at all boring. It is similar to baseball.

I have never played rounders in my life. I enjoy playing rounders, although I am no good at it.

How lucky the kids in this country are! I used to go to a private English medium girls school. We didn't play any particular sports. Even though we had a games class, the girls would sit around and gossip; the teachers didn't mind.

Girls in Bangladesh are not very sporty.

29th April 1994

In school they took photos of each year. Thank goodness I was present today at school otherwise I would have missed it.

One thing I found funny for the photograph, was that I was the only person wearing a polo-neck sweater; all the other girls were wearing sleeveless or cotton clothes. I think only the Principal and I were wearing warm clothes. No wonder the girls thinks I'm weird; I don't dress up like them, but the thing is, is that their summer compares with our winter in Bangladesh!

1st June 1994

I have private tuition at home for my exams. My private teacher helps me with my English. She told me I could speak it well, but my writing needed to be improved.

When I first joined my school I could not understand the language. I still fear that I might not do well in my exams.

I study late at night and wake up early in the morning to study. I don't understand the style of the education systems in my country. The education systems in my country seem very backward; I wish I had been studying in England from my childhood. Studying in England is like a revolution to my brain. When I finish my education here I would like to go back to my country and teach the people what I have learned.

24th June 1994

Exams are finished and I know I did not do very well. I studied day and night and still I did not do the best I could. I didn't go out, or watch TV, and sometimes I even forgot to eat.

If I tell my family that I didn't do well, they are going to be very angry.

When my exams were going on I took a rest for few minutes and watched the news on TV. I got beaten for watching TV. I will never forget that moment. Reasmine and Neasmine were out. If they hadn't of come home early I don't know what my mother would have done to me.

My mum pulled me out of the TV room, by grabbing my hair. I dare not scream from the pain, because the neighbours would hear, and our reputation would be ruined. She took me to my room and released my hair. I protested that I had finished my revision and I was taking a rest.

This answer made her more furious; mum scolded me and she used unspeakable words in Bangla language. Then she slapped me three or four times on both cheeks; she left the room after that.

That moment I was angry too. I got a pen and with all my strength, I stabbed my left palm. I could feel the pen's nib inside my palm; the blood oozing out. The pain was too much for me; I cried out loud, that brought my mum back to my room. She removed one of her blocked-heel sandals and began to hit me with it, all over my body, as if I was a piece of meat and she was the butcher.

My tears fell and she didn't care, to her it was like – shits!

Rave

The room was lit by a dozen candles. There were two long, narrow windows and they were patched with planks from outside. From inside these windows were covered by rag clothes not allowing any sunlight into the room.

There were more than 15 people in the room and the atmosphere was suffocating. A thick cloud of smoke hung over the walls. This smoke cloud was darker than a monsoon cloud, and smelled worse than industrial pollution. In this square shaped room there was no furniture except for the music system which was playing 'Eyes of Truth' from Enigma's album. People were laid out on the floor; as they slept they looked half dead. Others sat in deep meditation with drugs. They looked like a group of zombies.

At the far end of the room in a corner, Mark sat alone on a torn mattress, leaning against the wall. His legs were stretched out and on his lap was a packet of icy-white cocaine.

"Hey, I don't know if I did a good job for Sarah" said Mark to himself. He was talking non-stop to himself, as if somebody forgot to turn off the radio. "It is not my problem. She gave me money. Yes money! Lots and lots of money" and he brought out of his pocket some £10 notes. He began singing "Money, money, money, what so funny in a rich mans world". He grabbed the money tight and threw them in the air over his head.

Slowly it fell landing over him, like snowflakes falling from the sky. He was enjoying the scene. He was enjoying the money as it touched his body, and he said, "Do you know how I cried for these?" As he gathered all the notes, he showed them to everyone in the room. "My mum kicked me out of the house for this shit. My fucking dad divorced mum for this shit. Yes for this shit! I took drugs for this shit! Ah, ahhh, ohhh, ehhho!" suddenly he broke into hysterical laughter.

"SHUT UP! You son of a bitch", someone yelled at Mark from inside the room. Mark ignored the remark, he was out of his senses. Mark busily put away his money in his jeans pocket. He kept out one single £10 note. Then he placed some cocaine powder on the side of the queen's head. He carefully started to roll the note to make a cigarette with cocaine inside it.

This difficult operation was done with patience. Within a minute the special cigarette was rolled and ready. He popped the cigarette between his lips. He lit the cigarette with a lighter, and begun to smoke it. He inhaled the smoke deeply, he said to himself …

"You don't know how good it feels to smoke money".

In less than a minute the rolled money had vanished. Only the ashes were left in the ashtray. Mark sprinkled the ash into an empty glass. Then he poured b… in that glass, he drank it in one go. "The taste is exotic," he murmured through his burnt lips. And then Mark fell into deep meditation.

The seconds passed into a minute, a minute into days, days into weeks, weeks into a month, and months into a year. And that is the time when Jeasmine remembered lovely Mark. "What is the matter with him?" asked Jeasmine, as she stepped into the room and walked straight towards him.

"You made him very happy. That's the matter with him", said a fellow from the room.

Jeasmine sat beside Mark. She gently lifted his head from the floor, and placed it delicately on her lap, as if one false move of the finger would make it explode. Like a nuclear bomb. She began to stroke his blonde hair with her fingers. As she untangled his hair Mark woke up. He did not have the strength to move a single muscle, nor could he hold any conversation with her.

Jeasmine slightly bent her upper body down. Her dyed chestnut-brown hair fell over Mark's face. She wanted to kiss him on his purple lips. Instead she moved her mouth towards his right ear. She slowly parts her lips and sweetly whispered to Mark "Let us start our life again. I'll be beside you, and you'll be beside me, always".

Mark did not answer nor did he move from his position. Jeasmine knew he was awoken by her passion. She did not need an answer; his silence explained everything to her. The silence played the role of contradiction. He could never be rejuvenated. The horror of these thoughts made Jeasmine cry bitterly. Her warm teardrops fell on Mark's stone cold cheeks. He could not tolerate her pain anymore. He opened his eyes and looked above at Jeasmine's face. His hazel brown eyes met her dark black eyes.

"Who am I, what I am seeking for? It feels like I'm lost in a dark tunnel. Whether the tunnel has an endless darkness path, or whether the path leads to brightness. I don't know. I am just relying on my fate to free me from this curse", thought Mark silently.

He did not even ask why Jeasmine was crying. She was silent, not because she wants an answer. She herself was confused about her own life. She was stuck in the same tunnel, although she didn't realise it.

Jeasmine

24th Aug 1994

I'm still in one piece, and am not happy to go back to school.

I don't know if the new girls are going to tease me. I know everyone in school is going to laugh at me, when they see me. It's a shame no matter how hard I try I can't keep the knowledge in my brain. I'm just a thick head!

26th Aug 1994

I just finished reading a horror book today. The ending was very sad, I even cried.

It is a story about a girl who fell in love with a monster, who could change into a human. Jethro, the monster, at the end sacrifices his life for love.

I felt as if I was part of that story. I want to know Jethro in real life because there is no one for me.

20th Oct 1994

Half term started and my best friend Victoria, who is no longer in my year, had gone to school trip. I don't know what I would have done if she was not around to support me. It is only for her, I am still in the same school. Victoria gave me hope and encouragement. She really understands me.

Victoria is my true English friend. I pray that she lives her life prosperously, forever.

25th Oct 1994

Nothing exciting happens when my school is closed for holiday. Everyday, all I do is study, sleep, eat and watch telly. I can't even go out; all I can do is study at home.

I feel like I'm in a prison. I want to cry out loud. I have fucked up my life. The person I love and I want, I'll never get. Everything seems to bore me.

Sometimes, I think the reason I came to this country was to suffer in a place where nobody knows me. Why did I become embroiled in my parents' quarrel? It is us children who have to suffer.

31st Oct 1994

Halloween night, well every night is Halloween for me, since I came to England. My life is boring. All I do is study, and I get bored from studying nowadays. I study after breakfast, after bath, after lunch, after supper and then before going to bed; study, I study all day and nothing gets into my head.

My mum and sister actually don't see the way I feel. Whenever they see me they say "why aren't you studying?"; they don't believe that I had just finished my studies and am taking a break.

That is why I secretly bought a Walkman and listen to music in my room. If they knew about it, they would break my personal stereo and then me. They think it will distract me from studies.

4th Nov 1994

This is the first time in my life that I have seen a stage drama. It was a wonderful experience. The play was called 'The Beggars Opera'. If I wasn't studying in this country I would never have experienced that feeling. My family would never have allowed me to see this at my age if I were back in home. Thank you England!

19th Nov 1994

My family does not know that I play the national lottery. They think of it as gambling. I am not allowed to play so I played secretly, because I have a plan. A plan to run away from home, if I win with all six numbers. This was the first time.

2nd Dec 1994

I am scared of my exam results. I didn't do well at French, maths, and geography. I don't know what shall happen to me when my family sees my results?

I cried all day in school today and yesterday too. I am crying every single day in school secretly. I'm in a desperate situation. I need help! I feel like killing myself, when I think that my dad is trying so hard to earn money and I'm getting bad results in my exams and studies.

Oh! I feel guilty. My god I don't feel well at all. My chest hurts. The last two months I have had a fever at night; it comes on suddenly and by morning it is gone. I haven't told anyone about it. My family would think it is an excuse for not going to school.

31st Jan 1995

I had a nice day in school; everybody is being friendly to me. I feel very happy that now I have lots of friends at school. My dream has come true.

17th Mar 1995

'Red Nose Day'. This is the first time in my life that I have taken part in something like this. I had to bring four tomatoes for a sandwich. This is the first time I have done charity work at school, and it was fun.

2nd May 1995

Dad came to London after a long time away. My daddy was quite upset to see my health. My dad blamed mum, but I told him everyone behaves well with me at home and also at school. I am very happy. Maybe that is the reason I look like this.

30th May 1995

I'm so glad that my family let me go to Yorkshire for my history trip today.

4th June 1995

I really enjoyed my seven days trip to Yorkshire. I described the whole trip to my family and how wonderfully I had spent my time there. I'll always remember it. Whenever I will think about it, it will give me joy and pleasure.

Everything I did on the trip was a new experience to me. I'm glad I repeated the year. My only trouble on the trip was that I couldn't eat anything. I am exhausted from the trip and I was very ill last night, but I didn't tell my mum about it.

27th June 1995

I received an excellent result in my exams, I'm glad. I'll finish my GCSE by June '96. I'm proud of myself

We had a geography trip today, we went to Dorset beach. We bathed at Plymouth seaside and the water was blue and crystal clear. I have always seen this kind of seaside and beaches on TV. Now I can tell my family and friends in my country that I have seen how beautiful it is with my own eyes.

Close-Up Encounter.

"How come I don't see you anymore," said Mark.

"You wont be seeing me anymore, in that place" Jeasmine spoke after along pause.

"Not anymore, yes never".

"Why have you given it up" said Mark through his cough, "Lucky you".

"Why don't you give it up to?"

"I'm too late. Now I'm just counting the days of my death".

"O' don't be silly! Honestly Mark!" exclaimed Jeasmine.

A hot July breeze had been playing with the fallen leaves of trees. The sky was blue as the ocean. Everywhere the ground looks green. The blue sky has white clouds and the green land has the different colours of flowers growing from the ground. The clouds were like the oozy waves of the ocean. Beneath that imaginary ocean, Mark and Jeasmine are cruising. They sat on the beach, where they met each other for the first time. "Look, I can help you to give up" Jeasmine could not believe what Mark was talking about. All she wanted to do was give new hope to Mark. Mark sat on the left side of Jeasmine. She moved closer to his side. She stretched out her left arm, began to roll up the shirts sleeves to the elbow. There were five or six cuts, which were still healing. Jeasmine narrowed her eyes and began to speak.

"You see these bruises. I did them you know, I stopped taking drugs". But she did not tell him when she stopped taking them. "I did not do well in my exams because of the drugs. Everything I used to learn, I used to forget. I could never remember anything.

Sometimes I used to forget how to spell my own name. I got beaten for drugs. Drugs did more harm than good. You know how much it cost me to forget D.R.U.G.S?" she spelt out the last word, before telling her cruel story ....

"The first few months, when my body shivered and my mind was thirsty for the drug, I began to cut my left arm with a penknife. When the blood oozed from the wound I squeezed out toothpaste from the tube. I covered my wound with paste and began to suck it. I don't know what pleasure it gave me, because the taste was gruesome. Only good it did was that it helped my sorrow. The burning gave me happiness. Just to please my mind. When I am depressed about everything I try a different therapy. I rubbed an ice cube on my arms then I scratched with a compass. You know you actually don't feel the pain, because the coldness numbs your skin".

Mark was astonished to hear Jeasmine's story "How could you do it?" said Mark, taking Jeasmine's arm, touching the wound with his fingertips like a feather. "Don't you think it is going to harm your stomach"?

She closed her eyes tight, and then she started to laugh. She laughed till tears fell from her eyes.

"Oh Mark! What harm can it do, more than drugs? She smiled at Mark, and rubbed her tears aggressively with her palm.

That is one side of the story. The other side of the story Jeasmine did not mention. Although she was doing fine, with her 'fine' she still took it because she could not control her mind and body from taking it. She was only trying to help her best friend to give up. She thought that in a few months time, she would definitely give up, and learn to live life as a newborn baby. Will it be like that? That she does no know.

Jeasmine

24th Sept 1994

History trip to 'Holkam Hall' in Norfolk. I couldn't believe my eyes when I saw the mansion. Such a grand home, I couldn't find the right word to describe its beauty.

When my dad next comes to London, I'll take him there. My dad has always been interested in marbles. He would be fascinated to see 'Holkham Hall'. I would love to live in a house like that. Someday I'm going to build a house like that.

25th Oct 1995

I'm feeling very ill. I began to cough till my lungs hurt. I don't know what has happened to me. Reasmine is not at home, it is five minutes to 12 am. I am home alone. Mum and Neasmine are visiting dad and it is four months since they've been gone.

21st Dec 1995

I'm very ill. Whenever I cough, spots of blood come out too. I'm scared; maybe this is because I cough very hard.

My mum is here and I don't know why I'm glad about it.

Dedicated to beloved Jeasmine.

14th of February 1995, Valentine day, a day for the lover, a day for loved ones. Mark died two days before Valentine day. That is the day, when Jeasmine had a red envelope with Mark's news inside it. He loved Jeasmine from deep inside his heart, but he had no courage to tell her, until he had gone from this world. He was not a bold guy. He never kissed her passionately. He did not want to ruin her virginity, nor had he wanted to marry her. He knew if he married her, they could never have children of their own. Besides he loved her money more than her. Maybe they both knew why they liked each other so much, that is why they kept their love like a religion. The sadness of his love life haunted him day and night. One day he killed himself, not sip by sip, but in one flow. He jumped from ten-story building. Before he died he had gone to his mother's house to meet his mother and his sibling for the last time.

Mark pressed the bell and after a moment a blonde haired woman opened the door. She was wearing black leggings, a blue jumper with holes in it; it looked very old and the colour was fading away. The person who wore it was the ex Mrs Jones. …Mark's mother. The door was wide open and Mark's mother stood there motionless.

"Mum wont you welcome your son?"

"Oh, my boy!" she exclaimed and pulled Mark towards her, kissing him all over his face; she began to cry. Mark was all emotional too. He could not say anything. As his mother realised that this was no dream, but reality, she began to speak, "Mark, where have you been, I have searched for you everywhere". Mrs

Jones shut the front door behind them, "Look at you! What have you done to yourself? You look like a corpse", then she led Mark to a living room. The TV was on. Children's toys were lying everywhere. Mark's younger brother, Joe aged seven, was sleeping on the sofa. Another brother, Rupert (Joe's twin) and his sister Daisy aged ten were watching the national lottery. Mark was searching for Alice who was a year younger than him …

"Mum where is Alice?" asked Mark.

"Huh, Alice is not well. She must be sleeping in the bedroom. I'll go and find out", said Mrs Jones.

Mark sat on the sofa where Joe was sleeping. He began to talk with his sibling.

"Mum has bought a ticket", said Rupert, as the numbers were rolled out.

"She buys one every week. You know every week there is new hope," said Daisy.

"One day she is going to win. That's what she told us," said innocent Rupert.

"Yeah, one day I'm going to buy the moon for me" said Daisy sarcastically.

"Don't believe everything that mum says. She told us last Christmas,' we are going to have turkey', but we didn't".

"At least mum got some slices of turkey", said Rupert, trying to defend his mother.

"Yea……", before Daisy could finish her speech about their poverty, Mrs Jones walked inside the sitting room, and silenced Daisy.

"Alice is sleeping, she has had a fever since last week", said Mrs Jones to Mark. Then she turned to Daisy and Rupert, "And you can sleep here with me. You don't have to change your room, Daisy. Mark you can sleep in my room. You need a good night's sleep".

"Mum, it's ok I can sleep anywhere".

"No! My son you look tired you need sleep", suddenly she changed the subject, and exclaimed, "Oh! I am so glad to have all five of my children together, after such a long time. You don't know how much I cried for you. Mark you are my oldest son. Wont you look after your younger siblings? Please don't leave me, I need support. If I thought of myself I would have married a long time back", said his mother weepingly. "Promise me you will not abandon us. I have a job at a food store and they pay me well. I even get to bring home free food. Now I'm going to find a house for us. Together we all are going to live happily. Aren't you going to stay with us?" asked Mrs Jones. Without waiting for an answer from Mark, she went on talking about their future plan.

Mark had no answer for his mother. He didn't want to hurt his mother; instead he asked "Can I see Alice now?"

"Sure you can. Go straight through the passage". There were three doors in a line. The first door led to his mother's room, the middle door to the bathroom, and the last one to his sister's room. That door was wide open. Mark walked inside slowly, so as not to disturb Alice, who was fast asleep. The room was too small for two people to share. There was a dressing table, which was used as study table. Beside it was a bunk-bed, a small side table, and opposite the bed, a wardrobe without any doors.

In the room four people could never stand together. Books and toys were scattered everywhere. The top bed was empty; on the bottom bed Alice was in deep sleep. Mark moved slowly toward Alice. He pulled out the stool from underneath the dressing table and sat on it, beside the bed. He stared at his sister, stroked her black curly hair, like their father's. The sight of his sister made him feel guilty and upset. He thought 'how selfish' I was. I never thought of my mum or about my sisters and brothers, and how they were living. I was selfish. I only thought of me; like my father, I too divorced the family. I thank god for not marrying Sarah (whose real name he would never know). Probably after two or three years, like my father I would have divorced her too.

These thoughts made him weak inside. He got up and quickly left the room. He went to his mother's room where he would be sleeping for the night. There was nothing much to describe the room.

One queen-sized bed beside a small chest of drawers, another single bed next to a wardrobe and a full-length mirror fitted on the wall, facing the beds. The room was cold and damp. The cold atmosphere did not bother Mark, inside his heart was frozen. He turned off the single light in the room, as if it was melting him like the snowman under the sun. He sat on the end of the bed and took out a piece of paper and a pen. He began to write a poem in French, describing his feelings for Jeasmine. He wrote: "Mon Rever"

> "Cettnuit j'ai fait rever
>
> Je suis reve, j'ai ete avcetu
>
> Je ne suis pas, faete une vision de la passé?

Ou vision de l'avenir
Seulemoments peut assurer ca
Comme le moments a fait
Nous on les le nait separes de l'une l'autre"

He could speak French fluently but he never spoke it until the day his father left them and went back to France where he originally came from. He dedicated the poem to Jeasmine. Mark was left with no hope after seeing the condition of his family. He knew he would be no help to his mother; only a burden. He got up, walked towards the window, which was open. He took a deep breath, then got a cigarette and began to smoke.

Mark was not thinking rationally anymore nor would he ever again. He didn't know what he was about to do. All he knew was that he didn't want to live. He climbed the window and jumped from the ten-storey building.

The death of Mark left his loved ones with broken hearts, especially Jeasmine. She could not believe that Mark had done this to himself. She wanted to forget Mark; she did not want to die too early like him.

Jeasmine

16th Jan 1996

I couldn't go to school for a week. My mum has taken me to the doctor. My family's behaviour towards me is suddenly kind. What's wrong with my health? I shouldn't have gone to that place; neither should I have taken that stuff.

12th Feb 1996

I'm painting three umbrellas for my exam piece. I am using oil paints; the subject is based on Renoir's paintings. I used two modern umbrellas and one Japanese umbrella. Only the background is left to be finished.

My art teacher told me the umbrellas are done exquisitely. I'm confident when I finish this painting, I am going to get an A* from my examiner.

I couldn't get up from bed. When I coughed, more blood came out, this time following on. My mum did not send me to school. Instead she phoned dad and told him that we are coming home, this week.

I am not happy to hear this news. Why are we leaving like this when there are only three months left for my GCSE exams?

The Medical Report.

"How long have you been taking drugs?" the doctor asked Jeasmine.

"More than a year" was her answer. Jeasmine's mother was shocked at the news her daughter was revealing. Mrs Salmon sat quietly in the doctor's room, listening to the doctor and her daughter.

"When did you decide to give up?"

"Few months ago"

"Did anyone help you to give up?"

"No, I helped myself"

"Did you take this yourself or did someone force you?"

"Nobody ruined my life, I was fed up in my life"

"Now, Mrs Salmon, I am going to ask you some personal questions" said the doctor turning to Mrs Salmon, "Does your husband know about this matter?"

"My husband doesn't know anything, and besides he lives in Bangladesh. He only comes to England when he feels like it," answered Mrs Salmon, aware of the words she used.

The doctor thought he had heard enough, and he suspected why Jeasmine took drugs. Without wanting to hear more he started again with sympathy.

"Now, I am going to tell you something. You may not be prepared for this news" after a minute's pause the doctor began, " I really don't know how to break this news to you, but it is the fact, and I being the doctor have to break the news to you. And I am afraid I have to do it in front of you, Jeasmine. Although it breaks my heart to say it in front of you. You should know the harm you have done to yourself. It is the hard fact and sooner or later someone is going to tell you. It is best that you hear it now, and think what you're going to do with your life after this moment".

Before the doctor could give the breaking news Mrs Salmon interrupted him, "doctor can you please not discuss this in front of Jeasmine?" she said with a quiver voice of fear. As soon as Jeasmine left the room the doctor began without being interrupted anymore.

"She has a form of lung cancer!" he exclaimed, uttering those words with a single breath. After he had finished he drank a glass of water and offered another glass to Mrs Salmon. But Mrs Salmon was not in the mood to drink anything. She could not say anything. She wanted to open her mouth but nothing was said, when she opened her mouth. She thought she was dreaming, a nightmare waiting to wake up at any minute.

This was no dream, it was the real fact. Mrs Salmon realised the situation and said with a soft-spoken voice, "Doctor! Please tell me, all these reports are wrong," grabbing the x-rays and medical reports.

The two hours that passed with the doctor, were like an interview with a vampire. Mrs Salmon was silent on the journey home. When they arrived home Mrs Salmon sent Jeasmine to her room and called two of her daughters, "Neasmine and Reasmine where are you?" said Mrs Salmon raising her voice.

At once the girls came to the sitting room, when they all were settled on the sofa, Mrs Salmon began, "Jeasmine has lung cancer".

"What!" said Neasmine and Reasmine together.

"How can it be?" said Neasmine.

"Behind our back she used to take drugs", said Mrs Salmon, looking away.

"Did you ask her where she got it from?" said Reasmine.

"Yes! I did, but there is no point. She does not open her mouth", said Mrs Salmon getting annoyed at her daughters, "Stop asking me questions! O' god how will we face this society. Jeasmine has cut down our nose!" exclaimed Mrs Salmon.

Jeasmine.

16th Feb 1996

I said goodbye to everyone, I know at my school. My art teacher was annoyed with me. I was going away all of a sudden like this, without finishing my artwork for the exams. I told her that I'll come back within a week and I'll finish it. I promised. I also have taken homework from the other subject teachers too. I don't know when I was to leave the school. I felt I would not be able to return – no it's not possible. My exams are so close and no one can stop me from doing my exams. Even god can't stop me.

Besides my family don't know anything about my secret. Nor will I ever tell them. I have to come back to England and finish my painting no matter what. I am looking forward to how it will look when it is finished. I have a feeling I'm going to miss all my friends in England.

Wishing for the evening star.

'Jeasmine face the reality', said Neasmine who came to Jeasmine's room to see her, "what is the matter with you. You know mum and dad wont let you go anywhere at this time. You can hear yourself. They're shouting. They're having an argument about you. Besides you're too ill to travel, and going to London would be out of the question. You know it's for your own good. I really don't see the point why you want to go?"

Jeasmine could no longer hear, Neasmine was making her depressed with this conversation. Jeasmine opened her mouth but said nothing. Then again she tried this time slowly parting her lips she spoke.

"Why are you making me guilty?" she wanted to cry but not in front of Neasmine. She did not want to show her emotional side. On top of all she didn't want anybody's pity, when they do not even try to understand. After this thought Jeasmine began, "Did I tell anyone that I wanted to finish my exams?" lied Jeasmine. Every word of that sentence she pronounced gave her heart ache. She knew she was going to die soon, before anyone thought. She was dying to go to London. She could not eat or sleep, nor did she want to enjoy any kind of social life. All she wanted to do was to dream of London. Jeasmine never told anyone about these thoughts, but she didn't need to say it, because it was visible on her face and in her movement too; that told everyone. Her behaviour spoke for her.

"I'm sorry I didn't mean to hurt you", said Neasmine, "we care for you and we all love you. We don't want you" she moved close to Jeasmine hugging her, Neasmine began " we don't want to see you end up like this way. We're trying our best to help you".

Jeasmine was silent, inside her mind, she was thinking 'what to say next'.

When she came up with an answer she said coolly "Please, tell mum and dad to stop arguing. I'm fine, I'm really fine. You all don't have to worry. What is done is done forever!"

After Neasmine left Jeasmine alone, she thought, "I'm fine! This is what everyone tells me, and that's what I tell too everyone. It has become a cliché". Her mental illness made her physical illness worse. She had lost all her hopes. She did not care that she had lung cancer, the only thing she cared for was going back to London. Day by day she made her health worse by thinking of London. She could no longer take her life. She had no courage. She blamed herself for taking drugs. She was naïve. She did not know what she was doing at that time, because she was loveless and careless. All she wanted was a little bit of love from her loved ones. Does she regret what she did to her life? She does and she blamed herself for doing it.

Jeasmine.

3rd June 1996

I never expected my life to be ending like this. I don't know what wrong I might have done in my past life. For that I'm suffering now.

As seconds turn into minutes, into hours, into days, into weeks, into months, into years, into a century, I'm left where I was. Everyone is travelling with time but I'm stuck in the middle of a space. My fate does not change it is in the same place. Since I came to Bangladesh in February, I don't have anyone to open my heart to. I have lost all my friends. This situation made it possible. I've only memories to think of, though it hurts. I live in a fable world, waiting for it to become true.

I'm not feeling well. Oh! I've got pain on the left side of my chest … I can't take much pressure on the side. I don't know if it is the thoughts giving me pain. Suddenly, I hear someone playing flute very softly and tenderly. The music is very soothing. It is making me feel sleepy. It stopped, why? I hear now the dog barking. That sweet sound is gone. Just as my life will be, leaving the atmosphere cold behind.

Late at night, I'm just lying on my bed in the west room and I write this note: 'Numbness' I call it:

'My soul ask me – what is hope?

Can you feel it

Can you see it?

Can you wax it?

Hope is what: I am forgetting...

Mighty One, has wiped hope from my forehead.
More I hope, more hope goes far away from me.

Now I am frightened to hope for hope.
Where there is no hope to hope.
But still I hope...
Even though I don't feel it.
I don't see it. Nor I can wax it.

Parental View

"Why did you take drugs?" said Mr Salman.

"Just tell me what you didn't have?" and losing his temper he began, "I have given you everything that you wanted. How many girls in Bangladesh could go and study in England before they actually finished A' Level?" exclaimed Mr Salman.

This time Jeasmine realised it was about time that she said something. "Daddy, I am not saying that you didn't give us what we wanted. In fact you have given us more than we could ask for or need", she said politely, "but one thing we didn't get is 'love' from you or mum. Maybe in my case only?"

"Rubbish" yelled Mr Salman, "can you see love? You foolish girl! Why can't you be more like your other sisters". He had gone wild after hearing what his daughter had just said to him. Jeasmine was his favourite girl, she still was, but that needed to be found out. "You don't know how much you have hurt my feelings. You children have no sympathy in your hearts for your parents. It is a parent's dream to see their children grow up in the same footsteps as them or better than them". After a minute's pause, he began again, "You think you have seen the world. You are wrong! You don't know how much I have suffered to get to this stage. And it was not that easy. From a young age, I was ambitious. That's why I achieved fame and fortune. Why can't you be ambitious like me? You know if you want to live in today's society you have to build your on status", said Mr Salman arrogantly.

"Daddy please I hate it, I hate this society, I hate status and I hate your money," Jeasmine said angrily. I don't like this emotional blackmail!!!"

Both Mr and Mrs Salman were amazed at their daughther's outburst. He was upset to get this from his beloved daughter. When he spoke his intentions were meant to be good, but his daughter did not understand him as he expressed himself without emotions.

Deep in his thoughts he gazed, "why God, you've kept me alive to see this day. It is my fault I never spent any time with my children. I used money as a dummy for my family."

Mr Salman was speechless and his wife's face was violet with anger. She pushed the chair and got up; she moved forward raising her arm towards Jasmine and slapped her on the left cheek. Tears rolled down over her red hot cheeks cooling the visible mark that five fingers has left on her cheek.

The drama did not end there; Mrs Salman shouted in her daughter's face "You've ruined our family name! You selfish child! God knows what else you did!!! Today you are rich and comfortable and that is why you don't give any value to the money. Just imagine if you were one of those poor girls, who is dying for food. In this country if you are poor, you don't get benefits from the government, unlike in Britain, where there is no misery. Ah, I can tell you if we were poor and unfortunate then you would be unhappy too and have a reason to take drugs. But you have taken drugs just for fashion".

"Shut up" said Mr Salman suddenly, "Everyone leave the room, except for Jeasmine". One by one, Mrs Salman, Neasmine then

Reasmine left. Mr Salman was alone with Jeasmine, he started his conversation with his daughter. "Listen Jeasmine, this is going to hurt me more than it does you", said Mr Salman quietly, "Just tell me the truth why you took drugs. This question is going to haunt me, when you're not here".

"To tell you the truth father" said Jeasmine, "I took drugs....", in the middle of the sentence she was wondering, 'must I tell the truth, the facts or make up a story. I don't know what to say, what is the truth?' she said sadly. "…. Because I used to live in London where I was alone. Well it is not true, if I were staying here, I could have taken it too. I don't blame anyone; I got involved in drugs myself. No matter, where I was living I would have taken it, because you and mum were always fighting. That made me depressed". Then she started weeping and through her tears she spoke, "I really, really don't know why I took drugs, I've always been grateful to you. You have given me what I wanted. I don't blame you or mum, or anyone. I blame myself. You know there are some people in this world who have everything but are unhappy. There are also other sorts of people who have nothing but who are also unhappy. Other sorts of people who have everything are content with everything. The last sort of people who have absolutely nothing but they are happy. Please forgive me dad for what I said earlier in front of everyone. My mind does not work. I'm sorry daddy I wish I never said it. Daddy I wish I was not born. Then I didn't have to see this cruel world. When I was happy with my life, I began to die. What kind of judgement is this? Tell me", and she burst into tears. Crying and speaking to her father, who was stone cold. The emotions made him statue like, "When I began to love London, I had to leave. Why? Please take me back to London. I will be all right once I go back there. The English atmosphere will make me better, besides I want to finish my exams. I want to be a fashion artist; I want to be a fashion designer. I want to do something for this world", said Jeasmine.

Mr Salman did not know what to say, he could not bring back his daughter's life with his money.

Jeasmine.

16th June 1996

Tonight I don't feel scared. I'll write as long as the night will take me. I have everyone, though I have no one, still I've everyone. What I mean is simple: blood relations don't understand my heart relations. My family is treating me like a baby, as if I'll hurt myself, if I fell from a cradle. I don't need their love now. Where was their love when I needed it most? The thing is, I've never known what I am experiencing now, it would have been better if I had never known this. Or things I've never seen were one hundred times better than I have seen it. Time is the only wheel-chair that is making me go on.

There is no hope inside me, each day my hope is sliding away. It's like the waves reaching the shore and going back to the ocean again. My life has become a big ocean, where the big ships sink and only the dinghy survives, because they just linger with the waves. The funniest thing is, in my ocean the big ships are always scared to sail. Deep breath the ocean, there are old shipwrecks. It gives me pleasure to think that these ships will never be taken to the surface. They make me feel strong, once my ocean had been powerful. However, I want a new ocean with the big ships, but without a whirlpool, to drag them deep beneath the surface.

17th June 1996

Tears are in my eyes: every drop is breaking my heart. I wanted to be well known in my school for my good GCSE results, but I couldn't do it. I wanted to be at a good university, but I couldn't be there. I wanted to do good deeds for this world, but I couldn't do it. Now I can never make my dreams and desires come true, they would float in this world forever like the clouds in the sky.

I couldn't say a last goodbye forever to those I loved and mixed with in England. Nothing interests me here – Bangladesh. My only interest is London. Each day I hope to go back there. My life here has stopped.

Each day I used to learn something new when I was staying in London. If I had a wish, I would wish for a new life. Please god, give my life back. I want to live longer. Why did I take drugs in the first place? Somebody give me a life! I wish I could transplant my lung now. I cannot think anymore my chest hurts. Mark!

I see him standing in the corner and I repeat his poem for him not for me:

"My dream.

Last night I had a dream ….." I cannot write anymore I am dying.

R.I.P

This time a dinner table is set up, for four only. Father, mother and two daughters occupied the four chairs. On the far end of the oval shaped table a chair is left empty, all four of them are staring at it.

"I harassed Jeasmine, I ...." Before Mrs Salman could finish the sentence Mr Salman breaks in her confession with a loud voice.

"Harshness or harassment! You killed my Jeasmine, you killed her ... you abused her! That is why she took drugs. A typical child abuse case!"

Mrs Salman was silent it took her time to regain her thoughts. She still could not believe that her youngest daughter was dead.

"Why are you upset huh?" said Mrs Salman "It is only a daughter you have lost, you still have all your money. This wouldn't have happened if you had not sent us to London, it is your fault!"

"What do you mean my fault?" exclaimed Mr Salman angrily, "What kind of mother are you yourself? You were never friendly with Jeasmine. If I knew this would happen I would have sent you to Alaska alone."

Mrs Salman did not protest at what Mr Salman said, instead she began to cry and spoke in a shaky voice, "I was strict with Jeasmine, because I was only trying to protect my child, I was afraid of losing her. If only I knew that was going to effect her psychologically. I do know I have made a big mistake"

"Too late, for Jeasmine" said Mr Salman taking a deep breath and releasing it slowly, "isn't alive to hear it, but somehow it will bring peace to her soul, when she hears it from heaven". Suddenly he changed his mood and told his family angrily "why didn't you tell me on the phone, that she had lung cancer instead of bringing her straight here. You don't know how Jeasmine's death has shattered me. God knows, what people are thinking? I can tell you what they think, that we can't even take care of our children".

Reasmine could not bear to see her parents fighting, "mum, dad, please stop" said Reasmine quietly, when she had the chance to open her mouth. "Jeasmine was secretive to us, because we did not love her truly. That is why we could not find out how she got the drugs".

"Jeasmine could have lived longer if she was there, and you should have let her finish her exams. At least she would have no regrets after her death. She didn't die from drugs. She gave up heroine and cocaine, dautra, ecstasy you name it. She had given up and wanted to live a better life. Sadly she was too late, we all should have taken care of her" said Neasmine, who was beginning to spill more salt on their wound.

It has already been a year since Jeasmine died in Bangladesh. The reality of her death is painful for her family to put up with. Jeasmine was dead, and she would never fulfil her dreams. Only Jeasmine knew how she felt inside her heart.

The Salman family never knew any of Jeasmine's secrets. Where was that enchanted place? Who was Mark? Even Mark, himself was not alive to tell them. Jeasmine lived her life capriciously. Now she has become the 'capricious breeze'.

The End

www.ingramcontent.com/pod-product-compliance
Lightning Source LLC
Chambersburg PA
CBHW030149200626
46812CB00016B/1762